Hero Dad

by **Melinda Hardin**
illustrated by **Bryan Langdo**

SCHOLASTIC INC.
New York Toronto London Auckland
Sydney Mexico City New Delhi Hong Kong

ISBN 978-0-545-29263-4

Text copyright © 2010 by Melinda Hardin. Illustrations copyright © 2010 by Bryan Langdo. All rights reserved. Published by Scholastic Inc., 557 Broadway, New York, NY 10012, by arrangement with Marshall Cavendish Corporation, c/o The Chudney Agency. SCHOLASTIC and associated logos are trademarks and/or registered trademarks of Scholastic Inc.

12 11 10 9 8 7 6 5 4 3 2 1   10 11 12 13 14 15/0

Printed in the U.S.A.   08

First Scholastic printing, September 2010

The illustrations are rendered in Winsor and Newton watercolors and F pencils on Farbriano Artistico extra white, cold pressed watercolor paper.
Book design by Vera Soki
Editor: Marilyn Brigham

Dedicated to the children at Grafenwoehr Elementary,
Grafenwoehr, Germany
    —M.H.

For Grandpa Langdo
    —B.L.

My dad is a superhero.

He doesn't wear rocket-propelled boots—he wears Army boots.

He can't fly—
well, sometimes he can.

He doesn't have X-ray vision—
he has night vision.

He doesn't drive a super-powered car—
he drives a tank.

He doesn't wear a cloak that makes him invisible—
he wears camouflage.

He doesn't carry a laser gun—
he carries a rifle.

He doesn't have a sidekick—
he has a platoon.

Sometimes he has to go away for long trips, but that's what superheroes have to do.

My dad is an American soldier.

My dad is a hero,
my superhero.